Text & images © Imogen Knight
Typesetting © Ginger Fyre Press
July 2021
Ginger Fyre Press is an imprint of Veneficia
Publications

Joanna Javernick
Unsolved

WRITTEN BY
IMOGEN KNIGHT

MONDAY, 13TH MARCH 2017

7:36am

Monday again, the worst day of the week.
Who woke up one day and just decided Mondays should be a thing?

This is my new journal, and I know you're probably expecting me to say all those boring and basic facts about myself; like what colour my hair is, or my favourite things to do but I don't have time to do that. You never know when you're going to die and why waste it on something that won't be remembered anyway?

Although I'm not going to say anything cheesy, I guess I should tell you my name; I'm Joanna Javernick and if you're reading this, you probably already know everything about me. I bet right now you're acting like you care. Well, if you ever get to read this, I already know you don't care.! So, instead of wasting your time trying to find out where I've gone, do what you do best and ignore it. I'm running away in a couple months anyway; I don't want to deal with any more harassment. So, get ready for it guys because you're soon going to need to find another victim to bully.

Every day I'm mocked and villainised because I am not accepted by society. This is just because, as of last month, I'm no longer Joe Javernick; I'm Joanna. I don't know why, but that's when everyone started to despise me. I was, and still am pushed and shoved in the hallways, I've been threatened; someone even threatened to kill me just for sitting in someone else's seat, I have even been disowned by my friends. What is so wrong with me? I'm a girl trapped in a boy's body, and I feel I'm being outcast for it. I feel I'm being pressured into fitting into the traditional stereotypes, but that's not me. That's not how I feel.

Anyway, that's why I'm leaving ... for good this time. No, I'm not going down the street and setting up a camp in the park like we all did that time, when we were five. I'm actually going far away to another country.

5.49pm

I hate them all. Every day, I go back thinking it might be different this time, but I'm always proved wrong. I know that you are reading this right now, and one day I'll get you back. I no longer have the privileges of a regular teenage life and I hope you feel this way too one day.

~Joanna.

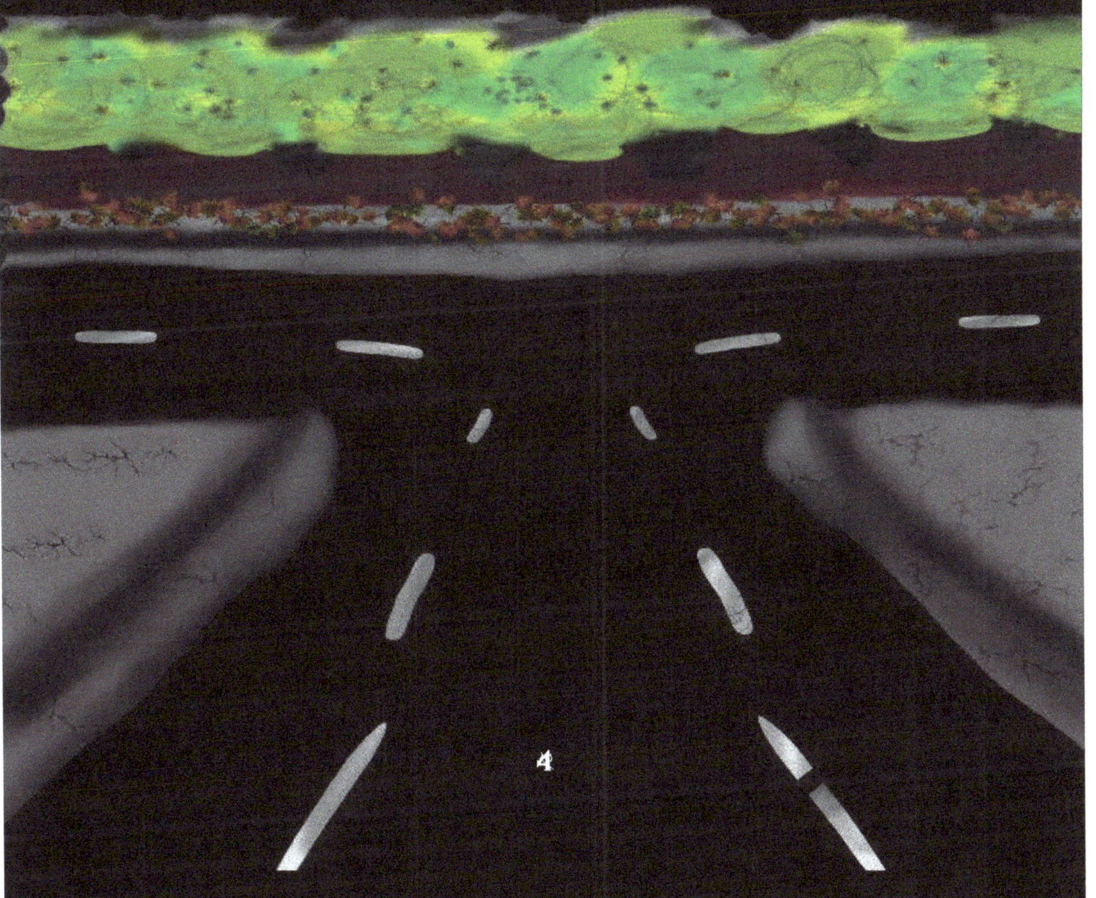

4

TUESDAY, 14TH MARCH 2017

6:14am

I'm skipping school today. It's pretty normal for me to skip Tuesdays, it's the only day when Savannah Smith is in school. She's the worst one of them, and I just don't have the energy to cope with it anymore, so I just don't. Usually on my days off, I just walk around in the park listening to the birds whistling while drawing random trees in my notepad. But I think today will be different.

4:27pm

Instead of walking in the park, I went swimming in the lake near the woods. Let's just say it won't happen again. I've never seen anything like it.

What did it want?

Let me explain. I dived into the lake, and swam for a while, just as any normal person would. It started with me hearing screams coming from the woods. They were ear piercing screams. It was as though someone needed help. I was mortified. I climbed onto the bank to get dry and dressed.

I will forever be haunted by the sight of it.

Staring into my eyes, was a dark entity, with the only facial feature being a smile; glimmering daggers lined its gums. It remained within the crowded trees, glaring at me from a distance. I was frozen with fear.

What was it?

After a minute of staring at the thing, I ran home, not stopping to check if it was following me. I didn't want to know, as I felt certain that it would harm me in some way.

I was terrified.

20 minutes later...
I was planning on not writing this next bit in here, but it's the only way I can tell my story. Okay here goes ...

When I got home, I realised it was here with me, in this house. I hid in the wardrobe, praying that it wouldn't find me. I know the wardrobe is the most basic hiding place for someone who is asking to get killed in a horror film, but this wasn't a movie; it was real life.

What would you do in this situation? I'll give you a second to think. Exactly.

Heavy footsteps pounded on the ground and my breathing became tighter. The groaning of its voice echoed around the house as the sound grew clearer and clearer... until it was outside of my wardrobe door. I didn't dare move as the handle of the wardrobe slowly turned and the door creaked open to reveal nothing.

Absolutely nothing, just the bedroom of Joanna Javernick.

I have an amazing imagination, but this was too vivid even for me to even think up. I'm convinced it's real, but truthfully it can't be. Maybe it's a ghost.

My mum would always tell me that whenever you have a nightmare, you should always think of the monster falling over. or rolling on the floor like a baby. So, instead of scaring me, it would make me laugh. I still do it to this day, whenever my nightmares scare me. That way, I can get on with life and act like nothing happened. However, I have such a connection with terror, and in a bad way, that sometimes it won't leave me, no matter what I do.

~Joanna

WEDNESDAY, 15TH OF MARCH 2017

4:17am

I can't sleep. After what I've seen in the last couple days, no one in my position would. Seeing something like that will give you mixed emotions about the world, and it's worse still if the things you see are actually real.

When she arrived home, I instantly rushed to my mum. She's always understood me like no one else would, but my story of the silhouette in the trees and the monster outside of my wardrobe, stretched even her beliefs.

I get it though; I wouldn't believe it either.

I had just got out of the shower and was feeling slightly better. I decided, it was probably my imagination, or perhaps I was just using these excuses to cover up the fact that it is real, and I don't want to believe it?

I've decided I'm not going to let this get to me, and to keep on going with my regular life and just pretend it didn't happen. So, I'm going to school tomorrow, and it will be like nothing happened.

~Joanna

SATURDAY, 18TH OF MARCH 2017

9:06pm

Let me talk you through my past couple of days. When I woke up on Thursday it was raining like crazy, so normally I would've asked my neighbour for a lift. Well, I think it was Thursday, I couldn't really work out what day it was. Every single device is saying something different.

My neighbours and my family are really close, but I get really anxious talking to them so my mum would usually ask for me. However, she was at work now on Thursdays.

My mum always had her whole life planned out: she finished school, went to university, and got a degree in medicine. When she came home, she met my dad and after four months, they got married and had me. But when he found out she was pregnant with a second child, he left my mum after forcing her to get an abortion with the first one. So, she had to stay home to look after me and wasn't able to pursue her dreams.

Sometimes I feel bad, as though it was me who held her back; I was so needy and too afraid to be left alone. I'm trying to change, and step by step I will.

Today, I was definitely going to be late, but I need this time to myself, even if it is just half an hour.

The trees howled like they were trying to tell me something: 'turn around', 'stay home today'. My imagination gets out of control sometimes, like my visions of creatures lurking in the shadows, or preferably the idea that one day I will wake up to find out I'm a celebrity.

No one was around on that rainy morning, which somehow made me feel safer. More connected to myself. But there it was again, the hideous mortifying figure. It definitely wasn't human; it was almost a shadow. But why am I seeing it again? It *was* my imagination, *wasn't it?* This time it didn't smile.

It just looked at me. The rain slowly slid down its face, creating the illusion of tears. I screamed at it multiple times, each time asking who it was but there was no reply. I ran past it, and I didn't stop running until I reached my school, arriving just in time for the bell. But no one was there: no students, no teachers, no cleaners, no one. It was midway through the week so there was no Inset day. I just went home. There were no more sightings of that thing, or anyone else for that matter for the rest of the day; even my mum didn't return home from work. Sometimes she visits my aunt across town, but this still didn't explain why there was *no one* around.

When I woke up on Friday it was still raining; it had rained all through the night. I wasn't going into school that day. I wasn't going to go in at all until my mum came home or at least called to let me know she was ok.

My morning routine was quite complex, in order to deliberately take longer and to feel more productive. I started off with making my bed while my shower heated up. It was the first time in ages I had made my bed. After my shower, I fried myself a 'English Breakfast' and made a hot tea with one sugar.

My living room is right in front of the window looking out at the road, so, I was going to just sit and watch the rain trickle down the window.

All was well until I drew open the curtains.

Once again there it was, so close to me that only the window kept us apart. It scared me so much, that, I jumped back, spilling my hot drink all down me. But even with the agonising pain of boiling water melting my skin, I didn't take my eyes off it. It was creepy how unfazed it looked, and how silent and empty the world around us was. That was all I remember, before I fainted on the carpet. Luckily, all the doors and windows were locked so it couldn't come in, even if it tried.

Next thing I knew I woke up and came over to my journal to write it down. Now we're up to date. See you next time for the frightful life of this Javernick.

~Joanna

WEDNESDAY, 22ND MARCH 2017

12:34 pm

I've been in hiding for the past couple days, but can you blame me?

These notes are not directed to anyone anymore, as I don't think anyone is left alive. I think whatever or whoever this thing is, it has either killed everyone or made everyone leave town. I would stay like this forever and grow old in this house, but my food is running low, and I don't know how to work a washing machine. So, I'm going to risk my life and go out to the shops down the street and find food and some sort of instructions. Honestly, how in my seventeen years of living have I not learned how to work a washing machine?! That's a question, with no easy answer. I just haven't!

Anyway, if I die it wasn't on purpose and if someone is reading this, congratulations on your survival. Also, can you put 'She didn't like any of you', on my grave? Thanks. I haven't seen human life in days.

I'm feeling so alone, frightened and depressed. I know, I'm almost an adult, but I miss my mum so much that I can't even put it into words.

The best I can do is, Mum, I miss you and I love you so much x
~Joanna

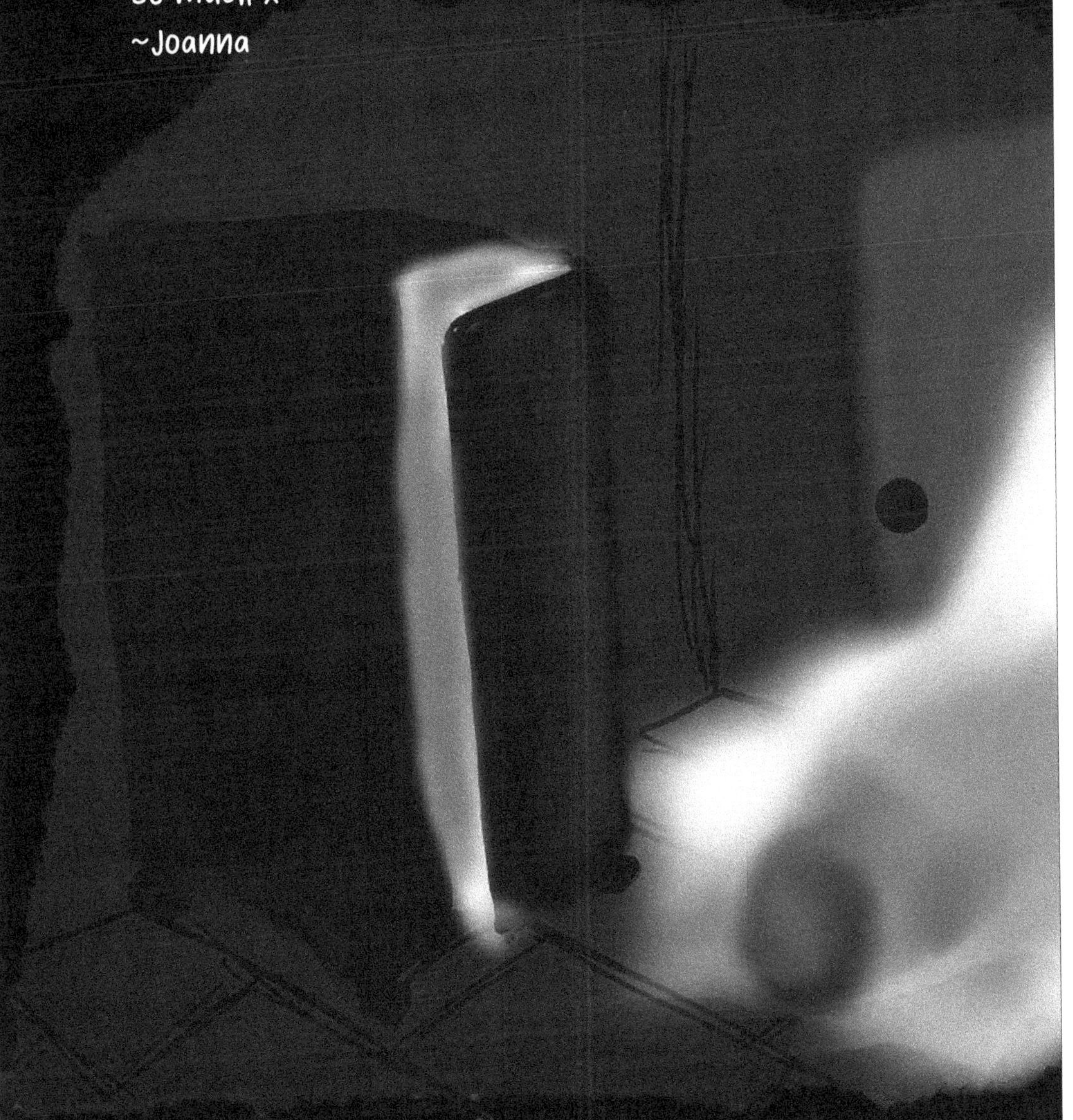

To J,

Please come back to me Joanna, you were gone too soon. I love you so much and I'm sorry you never knew your dad. This is all my fault and I hope you can read this from heaven or wherever you're travelling to in the afterlife. Please visit me and tell me your stories of the world. I promise I'll listen.

I will never forget your beautiful smile and how it lit up a room filling it with joy, and how that smile faded when you reached secondary school. It broke my heart and I know I could have helped you. I know I could have stopped it from happening. If I didn't have to go to work, you wouldn't have been going through it alone. I should have helped you. The memories we shared will always be with me. Like when we went to the beach on the hottest day of the year in summer and we bought some ice cream. I had chocolate and you had vanilla because, *"chocolate ice cream is so overrated."* After that, a seagull swooped down and stole the ice cream from your hands. From that moment, we both laughed until our stomach muscles hurt.

I remember your first day of school with the 'My Little Pony' backpack. Applejack was always your favourite.

When you came and told me you were no longer Joe, but Joanna, I was so happy and proud of you. After all these years of hiding who you truly were, you were finally able to express yourself. You left too young, Joanna; you had such a brilliant life ahead of you and someone or something stole it.

I knew more about you than you thought. Your favourite colour was sangria, as no pretty colour should have such a basic name like blue. You had an obsession with reading, but you didn't tell anyone because it wouldn't make you cool in school. Sometimes I would secretly buy you stories that I used to read and then hide them on your shelf, hoping that one day you too would read them.
See, I knew a lot about you.

I'm sorry I didn't give you any advice or was a shoulder to cry on during your most painful days. I tried, The truth is when your dad left, I couldn't bear to see your face full of disappointment, and sorrow. I couldn't bear to see you in so much pain. But that's not an excuse.

Now you're gone and I can't take any of it back, but if I could, you know I would. I will love you until the day I die. Hopefully, I'll see you soon.

Mum x

<u>Yorkshire police report.</u>

On Wednesday the 22nd of March 2017 at 13:05, the body of Joanna Javernick was discovered in the park next to Timber Lane. Reports show that the young girl was on her way back home from the shops with a stolen bag of shopping and a washing machine instructions leaflet. Bystanders reported that 'she was emotionless and 'frantically looking around for something'.

After that, she hastily made a sharp right turn into the trees. Where she was later found dead.

Her body was mutilated; all that was left of her was hertorso - her limbs were later found in the lake at the park.

The bones from her limbs had been removed and as yet remain undiscovered by police, divers etc.

Joanna's torso had all her ribs cut out and placed neatly next to her body. There are also over forty slices on the left side of her torso. All of her hair was missing, but no trace of any hair strands could be found. Her body was examined, and no trace of fingerprints were found that could have helped determine her killer.

All witnesses, and suspects have now been
questioned, and all of them came back
either not guilty or not helpful. They had
not seen any potential killer in the area
at or around the time of her murder.

We have no leads, no suspects, and no
evidence. We urge all officers to
investigate the case so that we can serve
justice to Joanna and her family.

We are worried that the case of Joanna
Javernick will go cold, and remain unsolved
...

SUBMISSION GUIDELINES

Submission Guidelines for those wishing to contribute towards future issues.
Stories must be either horror or thriller including: ghost, monster, demon, vampire, or anything else that you consider fits into those two categories.

They can be written and illustrated by one or two people; and in this case both names will be on the cover. If one writes, and one illustrates they will each be credited as such.

Stories should be between 2,000 and 5,000 words and can be in comic book/graphic novel format.
Highschool Horror is written for teenagers and young adults, and ALL contributors must be at least age 12 years of age. It is horror after all!!

Please keep stories clean, and free from abusive language.
All submissions must be made to:
HIGHSCHOOLHORROR@GMAIL.COM

HIGHSCHOOL HORROR

TEENAGE HORROR/THRILLER STORIES
WRITTEN & ILLUSTRATED BY
TEENAGERS FOR TEENAGERS

PLEASE SUBMIT YOUR STORIES TO:

HIGHSCHOOLHORROR@GMAIL.COM

GINGERFYREPRESS.COM

Gingerfyre Press is an imprint of Veneficia Publications

GINGERFYREPRESS.COM